by **Olga Koval, Daria Ermilova**

Space
Activity Book

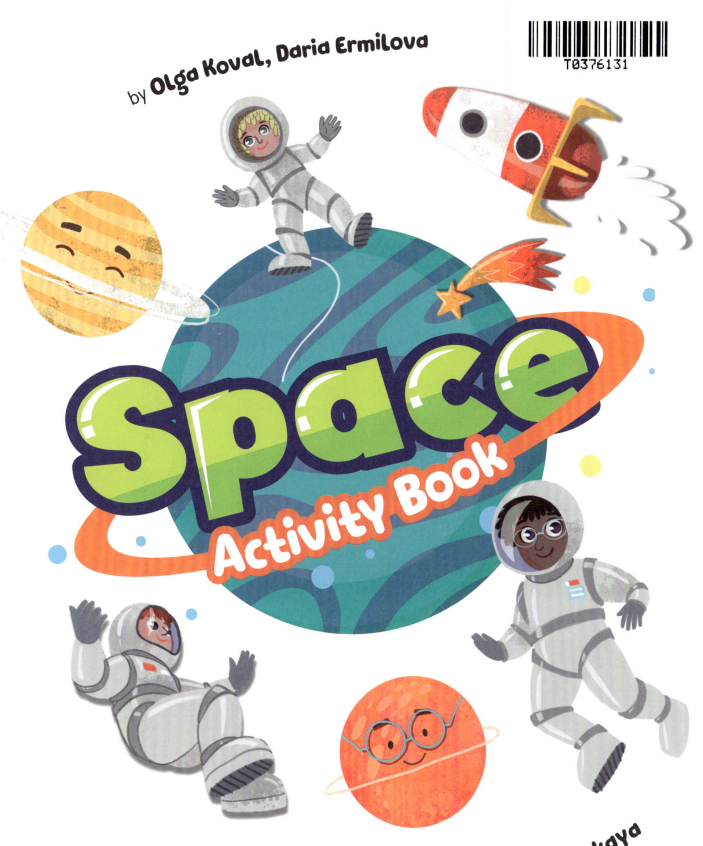

Illustrated by **Anastasia Druzhininskaya**

Solar System

Our solar system is made up of the Sun, eight planets and their moons, satellites, asteroids, and other space objects. The planets travel in an oval path around the Sun, which is called an orbit.

Saturn

Jupiter

Mercury

Mars

Pluto used to be considered the ninth planet in our solar system, but it was downgraded to a dwarf planet in 2008.

Sun

The Sun is the center of our solar system. It is a star — a huge, hot glowing ball of gas made up of mostly hydrogen and helium.

Light-year

In space, distance is measured in light-years. A light-year is how far light travels in one Earth year.

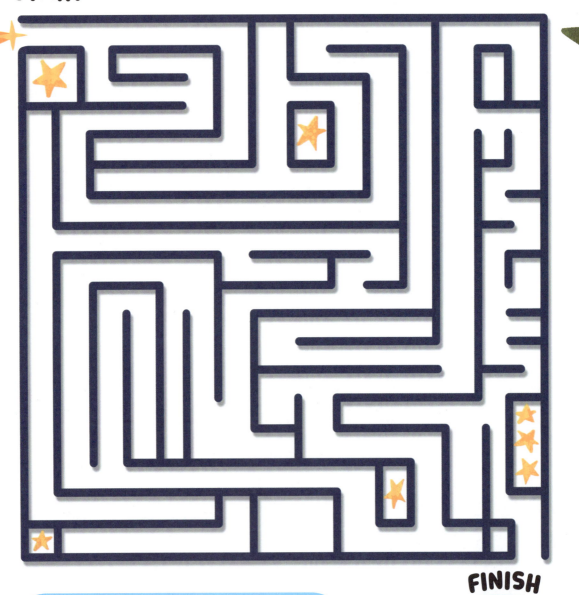

Find the correct path through the maze.

For extra fun, time yourself to see how long it takes you!

It takes sunlight 8 minutes and 16 seconds to reach Earth.

Planets

The planets in our solar system are made of either rock or gases. Mercury, Venus, Earth, and Mars are made of rock. Jupiter, Saturn, Uranus, and Neptune are made of gases.

All of the planets would easily fit inside the Sun!

Compare the sizes of the planets. Number them from 1 to 8, from smallest to largest.

Mercury

Mercury is the planet that's closest to the Sun in our solar system. It's made of rock and is also the smallest planet.

Help the rocket find its way through the maze to reach Mercury.

Mercury travels around the Sun at 29 miles per second!

Venus

Venus is the second planet from the Sun. It's also made up of rock and is the hottest planet in our solar system.

Circle the objects that are the same shape as Venus.

The temperature on Venus can get up to 900 degrees Fahrenheit!

Earth

Earth is the third planet from the Sun and is made of rock. Life on our planet began around 3.7 billion years ago.

Color the land formations green and the water blue.

Trace the dotted lines to finish the rocket.

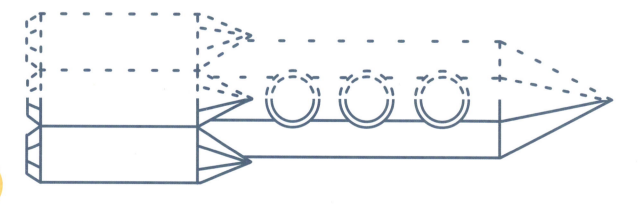

The Earth rotates (spins) on its axis every 24 hours. This is what gives us day and night. The Earth also revolves (travels around) the Sun once every 365 days, which gives us the seasons.

Satellite

A satellite is an object that orbits a planet or star. Some, like moons, are natural, and some are made by humans to study space.

Use a blue crayon to circle the natural satellites. Use red to circle the satellites that were made by humans.

The Moon is Earth's only natural satellite.

Phases of the Moon

The Moon doesn't make its own light. What we see is the Sun reflecting off the Moon. The Moon has phases, so it looks different in the night sky during the month.

Use a pencil to shade each phase of the Moon. Use the key below to help you.

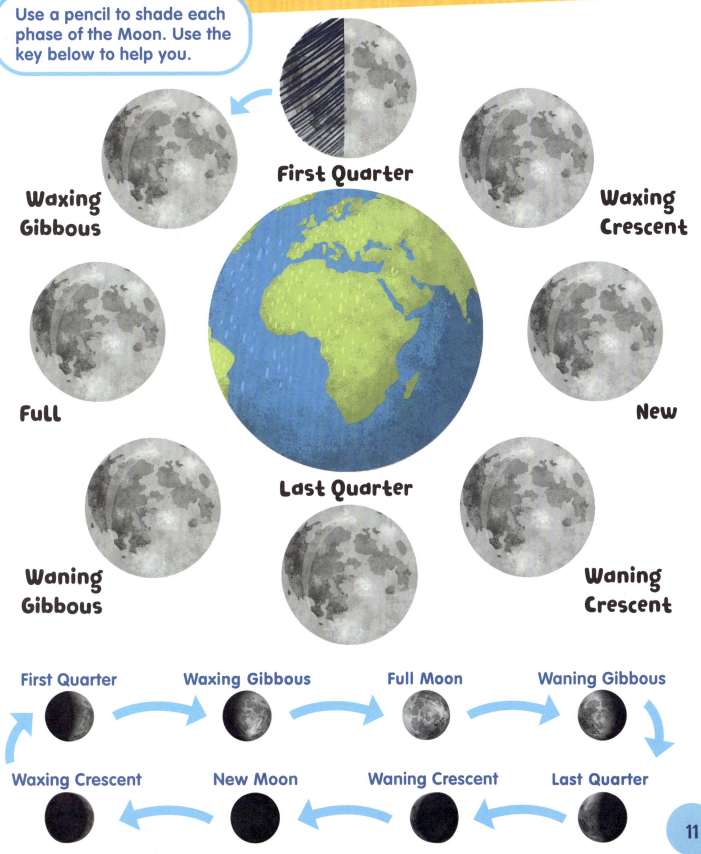

Mars

Mars is the fourth planet from the Sun. It's known as the Red Planet because of the red dust that covers its rocky surface. Scientists have been looking for life on Mars!

What do you think a Martian would look like? Draw it here.

Don't forget to draw a vehicle for your martian!

If you weigh 100 pounds on Earth, you'd weigh only 38 pounds on Mars. That's because Mars has less gravity than Earth.

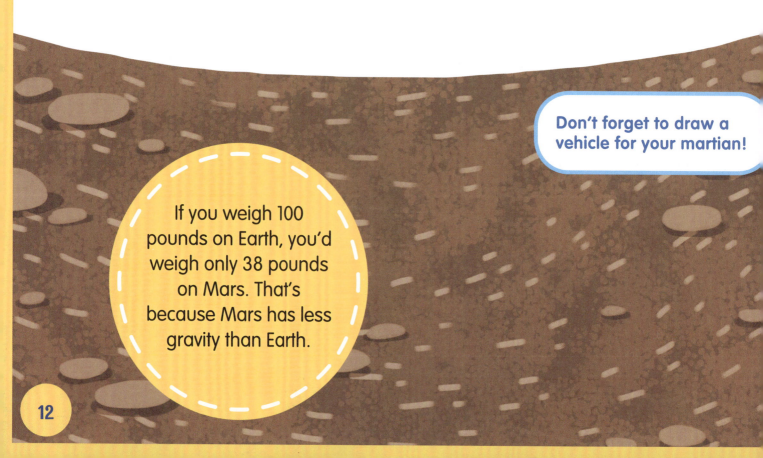

Mars Rover

Scientists have sent rovers (research vehicles) to Mars to explore its surface.

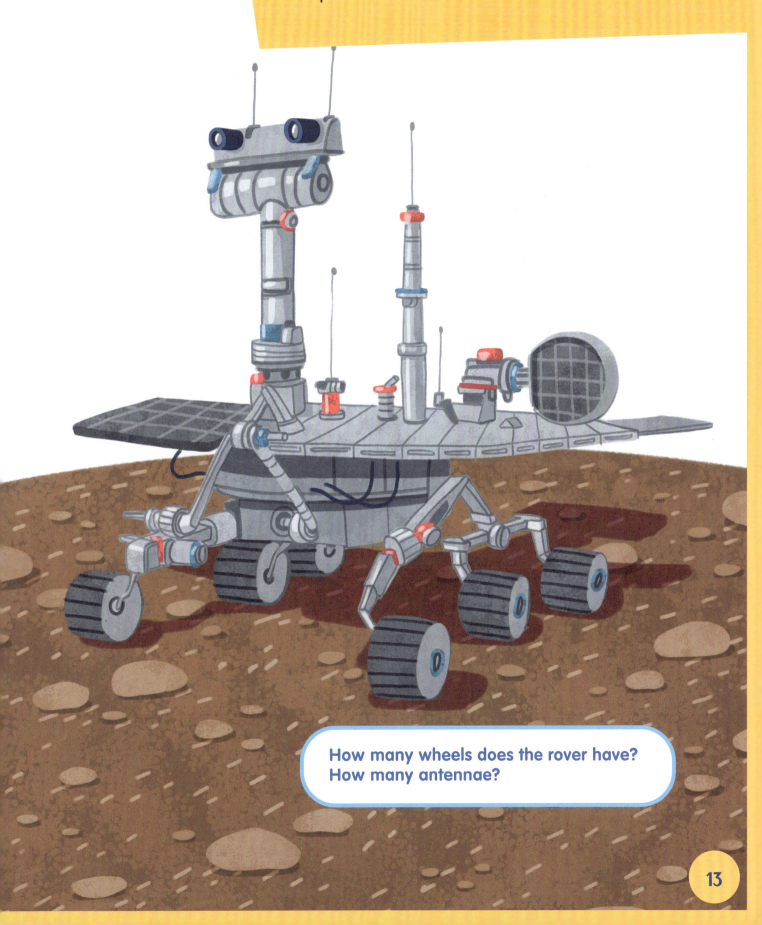

How many wheels does the rover have? How many antennae?

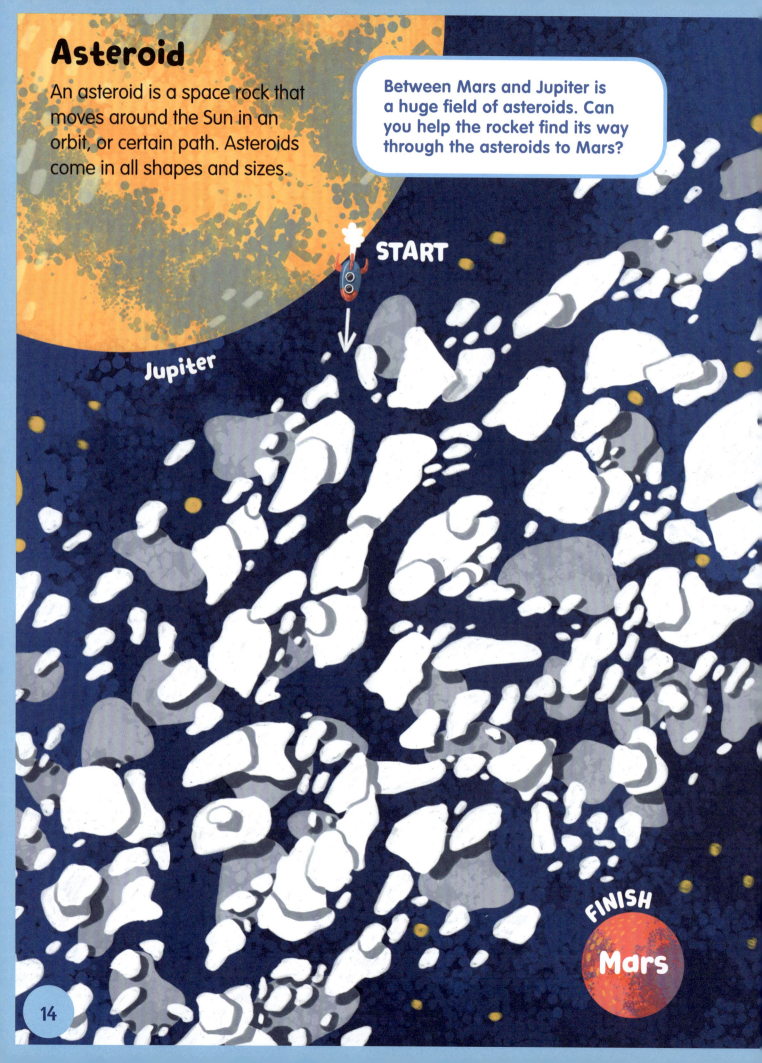

Jupiter

Jupiter is the fifth planet from the Sun. It's made of gas and is the largest planet in our solar system. All of the other planets would fit inside it!

Help the comet find its way through the maze to Jupiter.

Saturn

Saturn is the sixth planet from the Sun. It is a gas planet and is known for its rings, which are made up of ice, rock, and dust.

Find the shadow of Saturn and circle it.

One day on Saturn is only 10 Earth hours long!

Uranus

Uranus is the seventh planet from the Sun. It looks blue-green because of its gases and is the coldest planet in our solar system.

Find 5 differences.

Neptune

Neptune is an ice giant that's made up of water and gases. It's the eighth planet in our solar system. It has the fastest winds of any planet—they can blow up to 1,100 miles per hour!

On different planets, a year lasts a different number of days.

Follow each path to see which planet has the longest year.

2 — 255 Earth Days
1 — 165 Earth Years
3 — 88 Earth Days

Meteor

A meteor is a streak of light that happens when a meteoroid (a chunk of rock) enters Earth's atmosphere.

Circle all of the meteors. Hint: Look for the round objects with a tail!

Space Suit

In outer space, an astronaut needs to wear special clothing called a space suit.

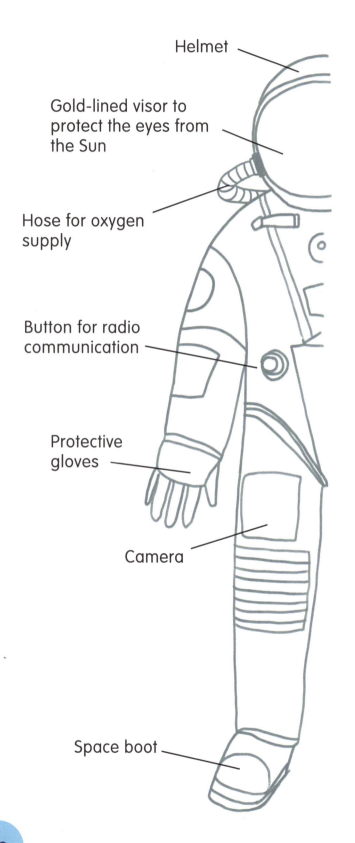

Helmet

Gold-lined visor to protect the eyes from the Sun

Hose for oxygen supply

Button for radio communication

Protective gloves

Camera

Space boot

Finish drawing the other half of the space suit. Then color it in!

20

When astronauts go into outer space, they are connected to the rocket by a special hose called an umbilical cord. It also helps the astronaut receive oxygen to breathe.

Follow the path to see which rocket belongs to which astronaut. Then color each astronaut's suit the same colors as their rocket.

Time to Eat!

Astronauts have to eat, too! Their food has to be stored in tubes and pouches, and much of it is vacuum-sealed.

If you were an astronaut, what foods would you want to eat in space? Circle them.

Telescope

A telescope is a tool that allows people to see objects that are far away. Scientists who study space use telescopes to look at planets, stars, comets, and many other objects in space.

Follow the path from the telescope to see what space object the astronomer is looking at.

Comet

A comet is a large object made up of dust and ice that orbits the Sun. Its tail contains gases and dust that come loose as the comet streaks through the sky.

How many pairs of comets are exactly the same?

Constellations

A constellation is a group of stars that form a pattern in the sky. One of the best-known constellations is the Big Dipper, which looks like a ladle (or big scoop). It's part of the larger constellation Ursa Major, or the Great Bear.

Count the stars that are part of the Big Dipper.

There are 88 constellations in the sky. Some can only be seen in certain parts of the world.

Many constellations are named in honor of heroes from myths and legends. Three bright stars form the belt of Orion, a hunter in Greek mythology. Look for them in the night sky!

How many stars make up the constellation Orion?

Connect the stars to see what the constellation Dragon looks like.

Rocket
A rocket is an aircraft that's made to go into space. It has four main parts.

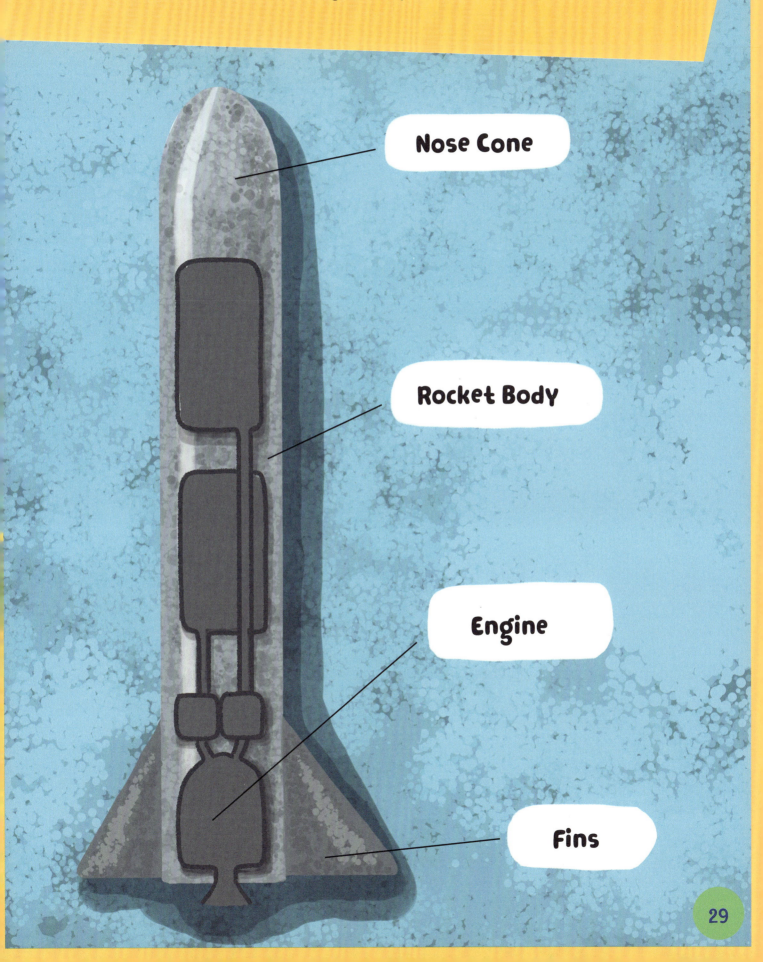

Draw Your Own Rocket

Use this space to draw your own rocket! Look at the drawing on p. 29 to make sure you include all of the parts.

Check out the next page to build your own paper rocket!

Make Your Own Paper Rocket

What You Do

1.

Turn the cup or glass upside down on the paper and trace a circle. Make a small dot in the center of the circle and draw a triangle.

2.

Carefully cut out the circle, then cut out the triangle.

3.

Bring the flaps of the circle together to make a cone. Add a piece of tape to secure it.

4.
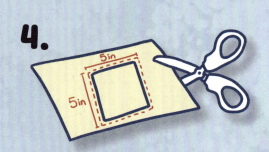
Draw a 5" x 5" square and cut it out.

5.
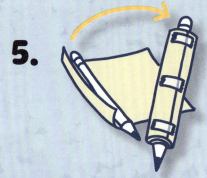
Roll the square around a pencil to make the body of the rocket. Use tape to secure the roll, then remove the pencil.

6.

Fold a piece of tape on itself so that it's sticky on all sides. Attach it to one end of the rocket body, then stick the cone to the tape.

7.
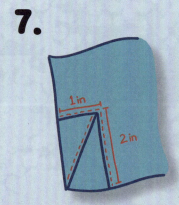
To make the wings, draw a 2" x 1" rectangle. Draw a diagonal line to make two triangles.

8.

Carefully cut out the triangles and tape them to each side of the bottom of the rocket body.

9.

Insert the plastic straw into the rocket body. Blow into the straw to make your rocket fly!